THE GOSPEL
Told by
the Animals

THE GOSPEL
Told by the Animals

Bénédicte Delelis - Éric Puybaret

MAGNIFICAT · Ignatius

To my little brother Bear

B. Delelis

For Isabelle

É. Puybaret

CONTENTS

A FAITHFUL DOG

It was a beautiful night. The flock had gone to sleep. My master, the shepherd, and I had kept watch over the lambs, and none had gone missing. I had been running all day, gathering in the ones that went astray, hurrying along the lazy ones who grazed too slowly. I hopped around my master, barking to keep danger at bay. And finally, I could nibble a few bits of well-earned cheese while my master scratched my back. I wagged my tail with pleasure.

Suddenly I jumped, blinded by a brilliant light. I rose in fright. I howled.

A man in glistening garments was standing before us.

"Do not be afraid," he cried out. "I bring you news of great joy! A Savior is born to you! Go! You will find a baby wrapped in swaddling clothes and lying in a manger."

We set off on the double. We hurried across the damp fields, once more plunged into darkness. I jumped in a puddle, splashing my master, but he didn't mind. Where were we going in such haste, in the dead of night?

BASED ON LUKE 2:8–15

A THOUGHTFUL OX

I'm an old ox. One cold night I will never forget, I was lying in the stable and chewing some fresh hay in the manger. My newly arrived friend, the donkey, was keeping me company. We were huddled together to keep warm.

Just as my sleepy eyelids were closing, I heard the big wooden door creaking open. Who could that be? A tall man carrying a large bundle carefully stepped inside. What was he carrying in his arms like that? Was it more hay for me and the donkey? Straw? No, nothing of the kind! It was a woman! The man laid her down on a pile of clean straw.

These were surely poor folk who had nowhere else to shelter for the night.

All of a sudden, a faint cry echoed in the stable. I raised my head, and with amazement I saw a baby! A tiny infant, pure and helpless. He had just been born! His mother rocked him, dressed him in swaddling clothes, and laid him in the manger. He must have been cold in the drafty stable, so I breathed on him gently to warm him up.

The door opened again and in came shepherds, sheep, and a scruffy little dog. In the silence of the night, they went down on their knees.

I'm just an old ox, but I understood. That child was the Savior. And he was born in my poor little stable!

BASED ON LUKE 2:16–19

A WOLF AS GENTLE AS A LAMB

The wind was whistling. The ground was bone dry. Not a soul lived out in the desert where I had taken refuge. Men had chased me away with their staffs because I had stolen one of their lambs. I'm an old wolf, and I was wandering and all alone.

I raised my snout. I sniffed the air and started to run. I could smell the scent of a man on the hillside. I spotted him and stopped. He was standing motionless with his eyes raised to heaven.

Little by little, I went closer. He didn't move. Then he turned and looked at me. But he wasn't afraid. He sat down and reached out his hand to me. I moved to about a yard away from him and crouched. Somehow, I could not jump and growl and bare my teeth at him to devour him. This man was as innocent and mild as a newborn, yet as strong as a giant. He was more peaceful than a still lake in the moonlight, and brighter than the sun.

He said to me, "The wolf shall dwell with the lamb; the cow and the bear shall feed together. They shall not hurt or destroy in all my holy mountain, for the earth shall be full of the knowledge of the Lord."

I don't speak the language of men. But this man I understood.

BASED ON MARK 1:13 AND ISAIAH 11:6–9

A STARTLED FISH

We were swept up in a whirlwind. The water was as black as the stormy sky above us. The current was so strong, my fins were no use; it was impossible to resist it or to dive deeper into calmer waters.

We fish had never known such a storm as this one on the Sea of Galilee!

I struggled, swimming with all my might, when a wave suddenly lifted me up and threw me violently into the hull of a boat. Splat! I landed in a huge puddle. Terrified men were running helter-skelter around me. I could hear them yelling, "Lord, wake up! Save us! The boat is filling with water! We're done for!"

And then, amid the crashing of the waves, rose a strong, calm voice. "Silence! Be still!" said the man to the wind and the waves.

And all became quiet. A great peace surrounded everything.

A fisherman threw me back into the water, and was I glad he did!

But ever since that storm I have wondered: Who was the man whom even the winds and the sea obeyed?

BASED ON MATTHEW 8:23–34

A FOX WITH AN EMPTY STOMACH

There was not a thing there to eat: not one hen, one fig, or even a grain of wheat. It was not a good day for a hungry fox. The sky was turning dark. A storm was not far off. So, loping down the road that leads to Jerusalem, I headed for my den.

Then I heard footsteps behind me—the footsteps of men. And I don't like men; they hunt me down. Where could I hide?

In three bounds, I disappeared behind some tall grass along the roadside. As the men drew closer, their voices grew louder. With my heart beating fast, I listened.

"I will follow you wherever you go!" exclaimed a young man.

Another man's voice replied, "Foxes have dens..."

I gave a start. He must have seen me! I peeked out, but the man had his back to me.

"...and the birds of the air have nests," he went on. "But the Son of man has nowhere to lay his head."

I liked that voice. I wanted to see the face of this man who didn't have a den of his own or any other place to rest. I crept forward through the grass until I could see him better. He was saying to someone, "Follow me!"

BASED ON LUKE 9:57–59

AN IMPATIENT SPARROW

I was born just a month ago. I'm the littlest of my brothers. My mother is still feeding us from her beak. We have to wait in the nest as she flies back and forth all day long to bring us food.

The other day, she was gone longer than usual, and I was tired of waiting for her. I wanted to fly like the other sparrows. I got up on my tiny feet and gently spread my little wings. Fantastic! I thought. It's child's play. I'll flap them just as Mommy and Daddy do, and I'll fly off into the clouds. I climbed to the edge of the nest and threw myself into thin air. Whoopee! I cried. For a moment, I felt utterly free!

But a gust of wind suddenly blew me downward, and my wings were not strong enough to keep me from spiraling toward the ground. Terrified, I closed my eyes until... Plop! I landed in a haystack!

A man spotted me. He took me in the palm of his hand. I trembled all over. There were other men around us, and some women too. The man said to them, "Not one sparrow will fall to the ground without your Father's will. As for you, even the hairs of your head are all numbered. So, do not be afraid; you are more valuable than many sparrows."

Then he opened his hand and gave me a gentle push. And, all of a sudden, I was flying!

BASED ON MATTHEW 10:29–31

A LOST SHEEP

My paw hurt. I had ripped my white wool on brambles. I was filthy from the mud. And night was falling.

I had been walking for a long time and had no idea where I was. I could hear dogs howling at the setting of the sun. Where could I hide if a hungry wolf jumped out? Frightened, I crouched down into a bush.

"Yoo-hoo!" someone called.

With my heart beating fast, I pricked up my ears.

"Little lamb, where are you?"

I knew that voice. It was the voice of my shepherd! He spotted me. He parted the thorny branches, grasped me, and set me on his shoulders with great joy! We went home together.

At the entrance to the village, a big crowd was huddled around a man seated on the edge of a well. My shepherd joyfully shouted out, "I have found my lost sheep!"

The man rose from the well and came over to us. Gently placing his hand on my dirty wool, he said, "You see, in just the same way there will be more joy in heaven over one sinner who repents than over ninety-nine who have no need of repentance."

"I am the good shepherd," he added slowly as he gazed at the crowd, who were hanging on his every word. "I lay down my life for the sheep."

BASED ON LUKE 15:4–7 AND JOHN 10:11–15

AN OVERBURDENED CAMEL

The caravan entered Jerusalem. The baggage was so heavy on my back. I had been walking since early that morning. Flies were buzzing around me, and the dust made my nose itch. I wanted to sneeze.

"Come on, camel," my master said, urging me onward. "Keep going!"

I entered the gateway known as the Eye of the Needle. I had taken only a couple of steps when—oof—I got stuck! Impossible to go forward or backward. The gateway was narrow. It was too small for a big camel like me, laden with sacks.

"Giddyup, camel!"

My master pushed and pulled, ranted and raved, but nothing worked. He needed to unload me. One by one, he removed the bags of wheat, linen, and figs that he had tied up so carefully. He was flustered and unhappy.

Then I saw a man pointing at me and I heard him saying, "Again I tell you, it is easier for a camel to go through the eye of a needle than for a rich man to enter the Kingdom of God."

"Who then can enter and be saved?" someone asked him.

"All things are possible for God!" the man replied.

And with that, freed from my baggage, I at last managed to pass through the gateway.

BASED ON MATTHEW 19:24

20

A MOTHER HEN

The life of a hen is no bed of roses, believe me. I have to watch over the chicks, feed one, comfort another, break up those pecking at each other. From morning to night, I never stop clucking, rushing about, taking care of everything.

What I fear most is the fox. When the sun is setting, I'm on my guard; it's usually in the evening that the fox enters Jerusalem in search of food.

At that time, I must urge everyone safely inside. But usually Lazybones Chick is asleep in the hay. Tubby Chick is pecking at his tenth grain of wheat. And Rascally Chick? He is always up to some mischief, like splashing about in a mud puddle!

One evening, as I was rounding up my chicks, I overheard my master telling his servants that an amazing man was stopping by on his way to Jerusalem. "He heals the sick and announces to everyone that the Kingdom of God is near," my master said.

The man entered our courtyard and sat down. Then some other men came and warned him that he was in danger. He looked at me and my chicks and said, "O Jerusalem... How often would I have gathered your children together as a hen gathers her brood under her wings, and you would not let me."

He seemed very sad. Then he went on, "I tell you, you will not see me again until you say, 'Blessed is he who comes in the name of the Lord!'"

BASED ON LUKE 13:34–35

AN INEXPERIENCED LITTLE DONKEY

No one had ever ridden on my back because I was still a bit too young for that. My gait was slow and not very steady. I was still leashed to my mother by a brown cord.

Yet one morning, some men came and untied me and said, "Let's go! The Lord has need of you!"

I didn't understand what was going on, only that I had to leave without even time to finish eating my sprigs of clover.

After trotting along for a while, I was led into a little square packed with people. Children covered me with colorful cloaks and strong men lifted someone onto my back. I didn't even have time to see his face.

There was a crowd lining the road. Men, women, and children were singing and waving palm branches that tickled my nose. Men threw their garments under my hooves, crying out, "Blessed is the King who comes in the name of the Lord!"

Who, then, is riding on my back? I wondered. A king?

I trembled. The road into Jerusalem was steep and rocky. This was no time to stumble! Me, the littlest of donkeys, was carrying the King!

BASED ON LUKE 19:28–40

A HOPEFUL ROOSTER AT COCKCROW

On the darkest night I had ever seen, from the wall where I perch, I saw people warming themselves around a big fire in the middle of the courtyard. I'm the rooster in the household of the high priest, and I could tell that something serious was going on. Men armed with clubs brought in someone they had arrested in the middle of the night. I saw him walk by with his hands tied. He didn't look like a criminal to me.

One of his friends was standing near the fire. A maid accused him, "You too were with this man, Jesus!"

But the friend shook his head.

My job as a rooster is to announce the dawn. Each morning, I watch out for sunrise. But that night, darkness seemed to have covered the whole earth for good.

Someone else questioned the man's friend. But he insisted that he didn't know Jesus.

I knew he was lying because he was afraid.

"I don't know him!" he shouted, denying his friend a third time.

At that moment, a ray of light ripped through the darkness, and I crowed at the top of my lungs: "Here is the dawn!"

Then I saw him. Jesus was brought out of the house and led into the courtyard. His eyes turned to his friend, who broke down in tears.

O friend of Jesus, my crowing revealed your sin and at the same time heralded the dawn of mercy.

BASED ON LUKE 22:54–62

A JOYFUL DOVE

The garden was silent that one Sunday morning. The birds could not sing because, on Friday evening, Jesus had been laid in a new tomb. Hidden in a cleft in the rocks, I, the dove, recognized him. Everyone in Jerusalem was talking about him. I knew it was Jesus, who was crucified because he said he was the Son of God.

I stayed near the closed tomb all Friday night and all of Saturday, silent and miserable. I managed to sleep a little just before the dawn on Sunday, and when I awoke at daybreak my feathers were damp with dew.

I was amazed to see that the entrance to the tomb was open! Someone must have rolled the stone away in the short time I was asleep. There was a woman weeping nearby, but I knew that she wouldn't have had the strength to move the stone by herself.

A little noise made both of us turn our heads, and we saw a man standing there.

"Woman, why are you weeping? Whom do you seek?" asked the man.

"They have taken away my Lord," the woman answered. "If you have taken him, tell me where you have laid him!"

The man replied, "Mary!"

With that, the woman cried out, "My Lord!" And she threw herself at his feet.

Then I too recognized Jesus! I observed his gleaming face. He had died, yet there he was before me, alive! In the morning silence, I began to sing. And, with a flap of my wings, I flew off to announce the Good News!

BASED ON JOHN 20:11–18

Under the direction of Romain Lizé, Executive Vice President, Magnificat
Editor, Magnificat: Isabelle Galmiche
Editor, Ignatius: Vivian Dudro
Translator: Janet Chevrier
Proofreader: Claire Gilligan
Assistant to the Editor: Pascale van de Walle
Layout Designer: Gauthier Delauné
Production: Thierry Dubus, Sabine Marioni

Original French edition: *L'Évangile raconté par les animaux*
© 2017 by Mame, Paris.
© 2018 by Magnificat, New York • Ignatius Press, San Francisco
All rights reserved.
ISBN Ignatius Press 978-1-62164-248-0 • ISBN Magnificat 978-1-941709-63-4

Printed in June 2018 by Tien Wah Press, Malaysia

Job number MGN 18013

Printed in compliance with the Consumer Protection Safety Act, 2008